Series 401
A Ladybird Book

DOWNY DUCKLING is an adventurous story in verse, in which Downy and Monty create great alarm by their exciting escapade.

The full-page colour illustrations by A. J. MacGregor reach a high standard of excellence and will make an instant appeal to all children.

For a list of the companion titles in this attractive series see back of this book.

DOWNY DUCKLING

Story and illustrations by
A. J. MACGREGOR

Verses by
W. PERRING

Ladybird Books Loughborough

From her little cottage window,

    Mrs. Downy Duck looked out:

Said " Oh, what a frosty morning!

    What a lot of ice about! "

Then she called to Downy Duckling,

　　" Fetch a pail of water, please !

All the pipes and taps are frozen !

　　. . . Wear your scarf, or *you* may freeze ! "

Off went Downy with his bucket,

    And his scarf about him tied :

" Come straight back ! " called Mrs. Downy ;

    "All right, mother," he replied.

Downy quickly reached the river,

Found it was a sheet of ice:

Wondered, while the Mousies watched him

Thought, " This *isn't* very nice ! "

Monty Mousie brought a hatchet

From the Mousies' Hole-in-Tree;

" Thank you, Monty ! " Downy murmured,

" That should do the trick ! " said he.

Then he took the Mousies' hatchet,

    Whirled it up around him twice;

Down with all his might he brought it,

    Crash!—at once he broke the ice!

He and Monty lowered the bucket,

    Leaning forward as they dipped :

But before it started filling

    Downy leaned too far and slipped !

Downy's legs shot out before him,

Up the bucket swung again !

Bravely, Monty tried to save him,

But his efforts were in vain.

Down into the icy water

    Downy disappeared from view!

Monty, hanging on his wing-tip,

    Struggled, but was dragged in, too!

Meanwhile, back inside the cottage,

   Mrs. Duck became alarmed:

Sent off Duckie to discover

   Whether Downy had been harmed.

Then she started on her duties;

    Swept the cobbles with a broom,

Dusted round, and fetched some logs in,

    Lit a fire to warm the room.

Next, to get the children's breakfast

    Mrs. Downy Duck began ;

First she neatly laid the table,

    Then she cooked a mash of bran.

Suddenly, a hasty knocking

    Sounded through the little house!

Mrs. Downy's heart beat faster!

    On the step stood Mrs. Mouse.

Mrs. Mouse had come to tell her

That her son was lost to view

Through the ice-hole in the river,

Monty Mouse was missing too !

Both the mothers, very worried,

    Hurried quickly down the lane,

Back towards the frozen river,

    Back towards the hole again.

Soon they met with Mr. Bunny,

    Told him all their tearful tale:

Mr. Bunny turned and joined them,

    Tracked the footsteps down the trail.

When they neared the frozen river,
　　First they heard the youngsters' cries:
As they came across the hill-top,
　　What a picture met their eyes!

Monty's brothers puffed and panted,
　　Pulling hard on Monty's tail!
Duckie stood behind and helped them,
　　But they pulled without avail.

Now the others down the hillside

Hurried, calling as they ran ;

Joined up in the line with Duckie—

What a tug-of-war began !

Then, with all the extra pulling,

Out popped Monty with a splash,

While the others toppled backwards

In the snow! Oh, what a crash!

Now they gathered round the ice-hole,

Gazing down with anxious stare,

Where, oh where was Downy Duckling,

Not a sign of him was there !

Sadly homeward all departed,
    No-one had a word to say;
Mr. Bunny took the water—
    Monty *couldn't* turn away.

Gazing sorrowfully backwards,
    As the others passed from sight;
Thought he heard a sound, or . . . something,
    Waited . . . wondering . . . was he right?

Up came Downy, bubbling, splashing

From the river once again!

None the worse for all his ducking!

Soon they scampered up the lane.

Caught the others on the door-step;

    Mrs. Duck, in glad surprise,

Flapped her wings in great excitement!

    She could scarce believe her eyes!

Soon she had the dripping children
  Warmly wrapped and growing drier,
Drinking steaming cups of cocoa,
  Eating cakes before the fire.

Then she gave a breakfast party,
  Thanked each helpful furry friend;
Smiled with happiness at Downy:
  All was well!!...... And that's
       THE END